THE ROBIN AND THE REINDEER

For my Robin - A. P.

HODDER CHILDREN'S BOOKS

First published in Great Britain in 2020 by Hodder and Stoughton
This paperback edition published in 2021

1 3 5 7 9 10 8 6 4 2

Text copyright © Hodder 8 Stoughton Ltd. 2020
Illustrations by Carmen Saldaña copyright © Hodder 8 Stoughton Ltd. 2020

A CIP catalogue record for this book is available from the British Library.

ISBN 978 1 444 95654 2

Printed and bound in China

The paper and board used in this book are made
from wood from responsible sources

MIX
Paper from
responsible sources
FSC® C104740

Hodder Children's Books
An imprint of Hachette Children's Group
Part of Hodder and Stoughton
Carmelite House
50 Victoria Embankment
London EC4Y 0DZ
An Hachette UK Company
www.hachette.co.uk
www.hachettechildrens.co.uk

THE ROBIN AND THE REINDEER

Rosa Bailey &
Carmen Saldaña

It hadn't
stopped snowing
all day.

Big, fat flakes fell softer than a whisper.
They danced in the wind and swirled above the
packed snow as it creaked beneath reindeer hooves.

A flake, bigger than the others, floated down
towards Little Reindeer. It came to land on her nose
and balanced there. The tip of her tongue darted
out, pink against the white snow. Instantly, the flake
melted away in a cloud of warm breath.

'You can't catch snowflakes!' her mother laughed.
'You should know better than that, little one.'

But this was Little Reindeer's first time
in the snow - her first year of being alive.
The snow was a blanket of purest white,
draped over the only world she'd ever known.

She looked around the valley.

She could trace every curve and hollow of this place where she'd first stumbled on wobbly, uncertain legs.

Little Reindeer followed the other reindeer
towards the forest edge as the bleak winter sun
sat low in the sky. The herd was moving south
before the weather turned harsh. Little Reindeer
could hardly imagine the snow being cruel,
but her mother said this would happen.

That it always happened,
                every winter.

'There's a cave,' Leader explained, as she trotted beside him. Usually, young reindeer didn't lead the pack, but Leader had allowed Little Reindeer.

'Do you want to help?' he'd said that morning. 'If you feel brave, that is.'

Little Reindeer hoped she could be brave.
She looked over at her mother, who gave a nod
of encouragement. Shyly, she took her place beside
Leader and they began to walk deeper into
the forest.

Little Reindeer looked up at Leader as they walked - at his huge antlers and noble profile. Legend had it that their leader was over twenty years old - older than Little Reindeer could ever imagine.
He was wise and steady and Little Reindeer loved him like a father.

She gazed up at the treetops.
The trees were so tall – taller than
Leader's antlers, even!

There was no sound, other than the creak of branches and the reindeer's cloven hooves on snow. Little Reindeer looked around. She was used to seeing squirrels and owls, even big brown bears. But now? Nothing. The reindeer were alone, but Little Reindeer didn't feel lonely - she had her family and friends all around her.

They passed a pine tree with a big knot in
its trunk. Little Reindeer was sure she heard a
small *cheep!* - but when she glanced over, all she
could see was an empty nest. Even the birds have
gone to find somewhere warmer, she thought.

Leader noticed where she was looking.
'They've flown far away,' he explained.

'Where to?' she asked.

Where could possibly be nicer than their valley?

'To the other side of the world. They'll come back
in the spring. Come on, this way!'

The reindeer carried on walking.
The trees grew dense. The shimmering moon
came out above their heads. Little Reindeer paused
to gaze up at it. She could just make out the
shadows and shapes on its surface when - there! -
a shooting star arced across the sky.

Little Reindeer called out in excitement, and looked around to tell her friends. But they had pulled a long way ahead. All she could see were their little white tails bobbing in the distance.

'Wait!'

She broke into a run, leaping over tree trunks
and frozen streams, but when she stopped running
to catch her breath, she realised that the little white
tails had merged with the white of the snow. Her
friends had disappeared. The black shadows of the
trees crowded in on her.

She turned in a small circle, calling out. 'Mother?'

Nothing.

Not a single sound.

Not a hoofprint in the snow.

She tried to remember which way the reindeer were headed. Was she pointed north or south? Little Reindeer had no idea. Her head sank so low that her nose touched the frost.

Cheep!

Her head darted up.

She glanced around,

but - nothing.

I must be tired, she thought. She tried hard
to think what she should do.

She wouldn't panic.

She would be brave.

Maybe in the morning, she'd be able to find
the hoof tracks again. She remembered some
wise words from her mother.

'Bury yourself in the snow if you
need to stay warm,' she'd said.

She found a nice, deep pile of snow against the base of a tree, and used her nose to dig out a hole. She settled down in it and knocked a hoof against the trunk so that snow fell down from the branches to cover her. Her mother was right!

The snow protected her warm body from the icy air and finally, the trembling stopped. She rested her nose on her front hooves, staring at the shining white moon until her eyelids grew heavy.

The snow did make a perfect blanket.

Cheep!
Little Reindeer peeled open an eye.
Cheep! Cheep!
And the other eye.

She raised her head. There was that sound again! It sounded like a bird, but Leader had said all the birds migrated in the winter.

She wrestled to her hooves, her long legs weak
beneath her. The moon was still in the winter sky,
but now it had been joined by a watery sun.

The forest made everything so dark.
Little Reindeer still couldn't see any hoof tracks.
The snow had frozen over now. She looked around
and tried to work out which way the reindeer had
been travelling in.

Nothing.

For the first time, she had to admit it –
she was lost.
Lost and alone.

Lost and alone and hungry.

She shook herself. *Don't panic. Be brave.*
She used her hooves to find some berries buried
beneath the snow, and snuffled them up.

Then she heard the tiniest sound - like a sigh or
a whisper - as something landed on the frozen
surface beside her.

Little Reindeer raised her face, but whatever it was darted away between the trees. Little Reindeer felt a flutter of curiosity and began to pad after it. Was it a sprite or a will-o'-the-wisp? Her mother had told her stories about them.

She saw a flash of startling red and gasped with surprise as a pair of wings blurred in the air. Little Reindeer had heard stories of these birds but never seen one for herself before.

It was a robin!

She padded closer, being careful not to move
too quickly - she didn't want to scare it away.
But the little bird watched her
with bright,
fierce eyes.

'I'm not scared of you,' the robin said,
ruffling his feathers.
'I'm not scared of anything!'

Little Reindeer lifted her chin.
'I don't expect you to be scared of me.'
'Good,' the robin said.

'I hoped you'd be my
friend,' she whispered.

His feathers smoothed down. 'Oh,' he said more softly.

'Will you be my friend?' She swallowed hard. 'I need one right now.'

He looked back at her suspiciously. 'Why?'

Little Reindeer had to tell the truth.
That she was a little reindeer who ...
   'I got lost,' she said, as her head drooped.
She waited for the robin to tease her
      or laugh. But nothing.

                    Not a peep.

'Well, that was a silly thing to do.' His voice was kinder now.

She dared to look up at him, feeling a flurry of hope. 'Will you help me?'

He flew down to a lower branch. She could see his little red tummy better now.

'It's very round, like a berry.' The words emerged before she could stop herself thinking out loud.

The robin followed the line of her gaze
and realised she was talking about his belly.
He shook his feathers proudly.

'It's very round and very red!' he agreed.
'Perfect for lighting the way.' His eyes twinkled.
'Wouldn't you say?'

'The way south?' Little Reindeer asked.
'My friends were going to some caves.'
    The robin hopped on the branch.
'Why didn't you say before?

Finding the way is
one of my best skills!'

He flew down and came to land on
the very tip of her nose. His tiny feet tickled
and she thought she was going to sneeze,
but she managed to hold it in.

She found herself going cross-eyed when she
tried to look at him, so she stopped.

'What are we going to do?' she asked, his body
bobbing on her snout as she spoke.

'I'm going to show you the way!
Follow me!'
He cocked his head to one side,
as though he was listening
to something.
                    Then . . .

'This way!' He moved his little red tummy in the direction of a narrow path between the trees, and Little Reindeer began to walk across the frozen snow.

'What's your name?'

she dared to ask.

'No talking!' he said. 'You're making me feel sick with all the bouncing. Normally, I'd fly, you know, but . . .'
She felt his tiny claws give her nose an affectionate squeeze.

Together, they moved in silence, the robin's
little red stomach leading the way. He was the
strangest but cleverest friend Little Reindeer
had ever known.

The two of them walked
on through the forest.

The robin sat on Little Reindeer's nose, his gaze flickering between the weak rising sun in the west, and the maze of trees. He steered them left, right, left a bit more. All Little Reindeer had to do was keep walking. They zigzagged between pine trees and over rocks, Little Reindeer's hooves tracking prints in the snow.

They arrived at the edge of a great frozen lake.
Little Reindeer lowered her head to the ice,
and there was her reflection.

She blinked once, twice.
Shook her head slightly.
Blinked again.
'I look as though I have a red nose!'
she said in awe.

The robin laughed.
'I look as though I have antlers.'

Little Reindeer looked again - he was right.
She was starting to grow antlers - small, furry
nubs of things. Nothing like Leader's. Not yet.
'I'm becoming a real reindeer,'
she whispered.

'Hold on.' The robin fluttered his wings and lifted into the air. Little Reindeer watched the little patch of red streak above the treetops as her friend went for a bird's-eye view of the forest. Then he swooped back down. 'Caves, you say? I can see the way.'
He hovered in the air, watching her.
'But you'll need to be brave.'

'I can do that,' Little Reindeer said, but she could hear the tremor in her voice.

The robin's wings fluttered. 'Are you sure?'

'As sure as anything I've felt in my life.' She
concentrated on stopping the quivering in her knees.
    The robin hopped on to the very tip of her nose.
'Start walking.' He was very good at giving orders.
    Little Reindeer put one hoof in front of the other.
One . . .
After the other . . .
One.
Step.
At.
A.
Time.
All I have to do, she told herself,
is trust my friend.

She felt her heart settle. Her body lifted. And
before she knew it, her little hooves paddled through
the air as her nose shimmered. The red feathers of
the robin's breast lit the way and she was

She was flying!

She arched her neck to look around. The moon
was round and luminous, reflecting in the lake,
where she could see herself flying almost as fast
as a shooting star.

Little Reindeer looked down and saw much more than the valley she'd been born in.

She could glimpse the curves and arcs, mountains and rivers of a whole new world.

'Why didn't anyone tell me?' she gasped. 'I never knew this was all out here, waiting for me.'

The robin dipped his head. 'Oh, the world is very big,' he said wisely. 'But it's all yours - if you're brave enough to find it.'

Little Reindeer did feel brave!
A whole big world for a little
reindeer to explore. She found
her body was trembling.

Not with the cold.
And not with fear.
It was the power of her heart,
thundering inside her. She opened
her mouth to thank the robin but—

'Look down there!' he cheeped.
Far below, she glimpsed a small, dark shape -
almost like the opening of a cave.

'Look, hoof prints!' There was a trail
in the snow, where not one but lots of
reindeer had walked.

A snowflake landed on the little robin's head and she used the warmth of her breath to melt it away for him. He shook out his feathers and launched himself into the air, flying in circles above her head as they approached the caves.

Cheep! Cheep!

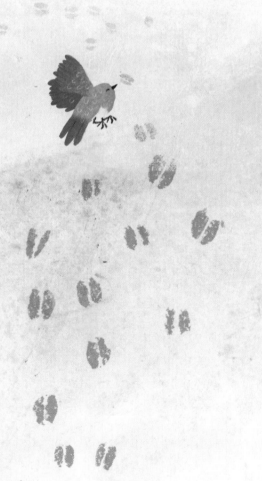

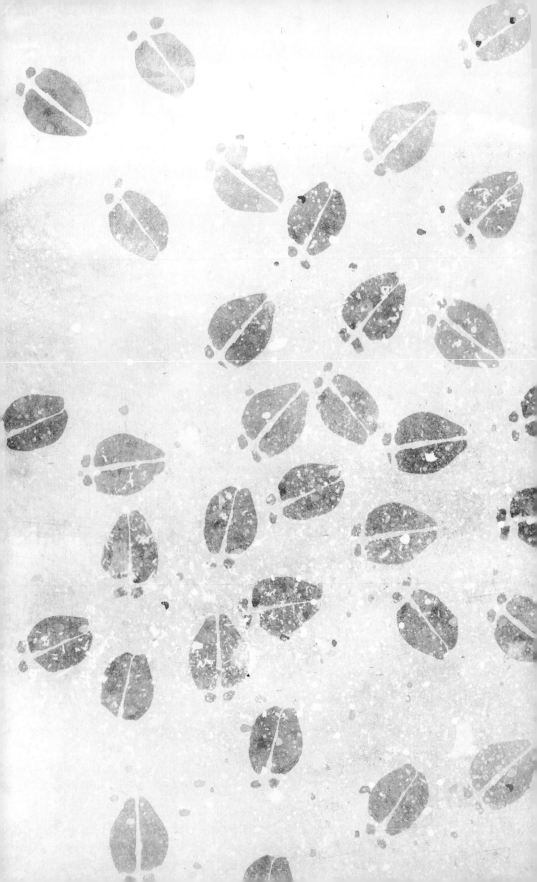

Little Reindeer dipped her head and drifted towards the ground until her hooves sank into the snow. Her whole body jarred and she began to trot, making her own marks.

The robin was singing, alerting the others to their approach. Little Reindeer kept her gaze fixed on the cave mouth, hoping more than anything that she'd found her mother and friends.

A face appeared against the black cave mouth and then another and before she knew it, a reindeer was racing across the snow to greet her.

'Little Reindeer!'
It was her mother,
welcoming her brave
reindeer back to the herd.

They touched noses.

'We were so worried about you,' her mother said. She drew back to gaze into Little Reindeer's face. 'How did you find us?'

Little Reindeer glanced up into the sky to point out her friend, but for the first time all day there was no flash of red. No new friend by her side. She turned in a circle, staring up at the faint stars.

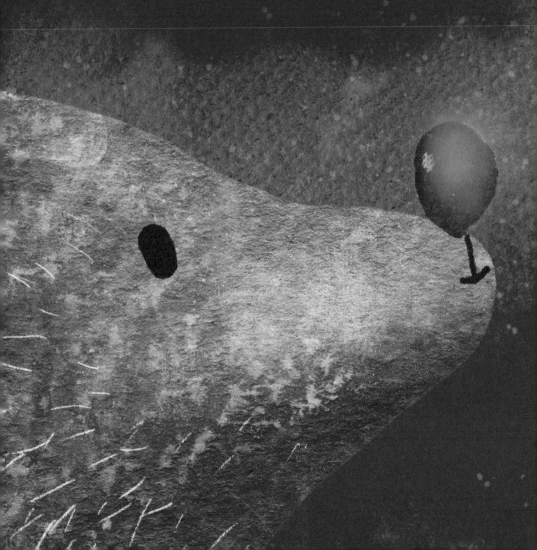

Her friend had gone.

'I never did find out your name,' she said into the emptiness. She felt tears brimming at her eyes.

But then there was a flash of colour across the sky. Lights blazed through the silent air in a river of colour – purple, green, yellow . . . red. The snow continued to fall and a huge flake landed on the tip of Little Reindeer's nose, lit red by the light in the sky. She held her breath, watching the robin's goodbye.

You're brave, she heard him say again.
The bravest reindeer I know.

Little Reindeer and her mother turned towards
their herd.

Leader watched her face closely as she drew up
before him.

'I got lost,' she explained, but she didn't break her gaze from his wise eyes. He nodded once, as though in deep understanding.

'And then you found us,' he said.

Little Reindeer glanced up at the lights as they flashed across the sky. 'With some help from a friend.' She squeezed her eyes tight shut and felt a single word pierce the air.

Goodbye.

A final flash of colour lit up the sky, red as a robin's breast. In the far distance, Little Reindeer thought she saw a tiny flutter of feathers, heading out alone.

Be brave, came the message back. *Light the way.*

Little Reindeer dipped her head in understanding and saw a faint halo of red against the glittering white snow. Her brilliant red nose, lighting the way.

Had it come from the robin or from deep inside herself? Impossible to tell.

Head held high, Little Reindeer led her family into the cave and out of the snow.